Story and pictures
by

HARRY JAPPAN

THE ADVENTURES OF

DINK. NOSE

Pink Nose is a cat, he loves to giggle and his nose is pink.

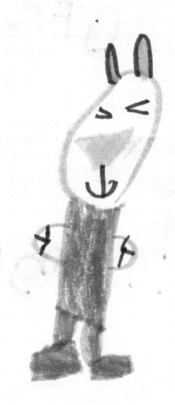

One day, Pink Nose came to an ice cream shop, he wanted to buy some ice cream.

He chose the chocolate
flavour.

It was a hot day, the ice
cream started to melt.

A rat came along and had
some ice cream.

He finished his ice cream and walked up the stairs to his house. He then went to his back garden to get his car.

He got in his car and drove to the playground.

The playground has a slide,
climbing ladders and a see
saw that made a squeaky
sound.

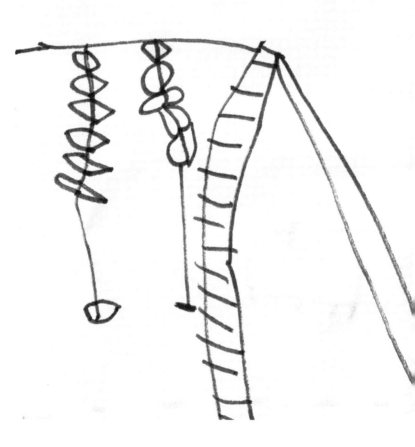

Pink Nose had a lot of fun at the playground.

After that, he drove home.

It is now night time and Pink Nose is at home and getting ready for bed.

While he was sleeping, he had a dream.

In his dream, he was in a video game.

He climbed down the stairs and saw a skeleton, a pink dinosaur, a staff, some gold coins and a few treasure chests.

He needs to find the key
to open the treasure
chests.

After that, he counted
from 10 to 1 and he went
to another place.

This time, he found a big red diamond in a forest. He also found his brother's hat sitting on top of a palm tree.

Pink Nose gets on a ship and he saw a shark and another ship coming towards him. It was his brother, Black Knight.

Black Knight said, "Shall we go on a treasure hunt together?"

Pink Nose said, "Of course!"

They found the treasure
and dug a big hole and
created a big pile of dirt.

After all of their hard
work, they found two
beautiful diamond rings.

They took their
treasures home and had
a good night sleep.

This story was created by Harry Lappan on 27 November 2019, when he was 4.5 years old.

The Adventures of Pink Nose

Cover and internal illustration by Harry Lappan

First published in Australia in July 2020
Reprinted in April 2021

Printed and bound in Australia